# AS YOU LIKE IT

Retold by **Jenny Oldfield**

Illustrated by Serena Curmi

A & C Black • London

First published 2009 by
A & C Black Publishers Ltd
36 Soho Square, London, W1D 3QY

www.acblack.com

ISBN 978 1 4081 0473 6

A CIP catalogue for this book is available from the British Library.

Printed and bound in Great Britain
by CPI Cox & Wyman, Reading, RG1 8EX.

# Contents

# List of characters

Touchstone, *a comedian*
Duke Senior, *living in exile*
Duke Fred, *brother to Duke Senior*
Orlando, *Son of Roland de Boys*
Oliver, *Orlando's brother*
Rosalind (Jamie), *daughter of Duke Senior*
Celia (Summer), *daughter of Duke Fred*
Jaques, *attendant of Duke Senior*
Amiens, *attendant of Duke Senior*
Adam, *attendant of Orlando*
Corin, *a shepherd*
Silvius, *a shepherd*
Phebe, *a shepherdess*
Audrey, *a goat herder*
Killer Karl, *a wrestler*

# Act One
# Going Green

10

It's the must-see match of the year – the fight between Killer Karl and Kid Orlando. But nobody is putting money on the Kid, who is half the size of Killer Karl and has never been in a wrestling ring in his life.

Here's the story. Listen up.

It's classic soap-opera stuff. Kid Orlando's dad was Mr Big around here, but when he died, his power and money passed to Orlando's brother Oliver, and big bro wasn't into sharing. He took everything and Orlando got nothing. Big fat zero.

So big bro and Orlando are smack in the middle of this major feud, when the Kid starts to fancy his chances in the wrestling ring, like he has to big himself up in front of Oliver, or something.

What's the point of that? you might ask.

I don't get it, either. But I'm only a comedian, so what do I know? They call me Touchstone.

But this is where it starts to get interesting.

Big bro now has a lot of pull, so he takes Karl to one side and tells him to pin Orlando in a corner then go in for the kill – no faking, the real thing.

Not a lot of people know this fight is fixed, but nothing gets by me. I stand in the shadows and listen hard. It wasn't rocket science for me to realise that Orlando has no chance of coming out of that ring alive.

So far so bad. But then the girls come into the picture and it gets much worse.

I'm talking about Rosalind and Celia. They're cousins and they're innocent victims, caught slap bang in the middle of yet more family feuding.

What is it with these high rollers? Once you have lottery-style money, you start to argue – but not the girls. Oh no, they're best mates. It's 'sweet coz' this and 'dear Roz' that. This time it's the oldies who can't agree. But more about that later. Here come the girls now. Watch this...

*Celia*: C'mon, Roz, look on the bright side.

*Rosalind*: Easy for you to say. *Your* father hasn't been kicked out of the city for good, like mine. Now he's holed up out in the forest, and I don't get to see him any more.

*Celia*: I know, and it's all my dad's fault. He's the one who did the dirty on him. But don't worry, I'm on your side. Honestly, Roz, everything I have is yours. We'll share it all – promise!

*Rosalind* (sighs then smiles): OK, thanks. And I know there's no point feeling sorry for myself, so I'll toughen up. What shall we do then – go looking for fit boys?

*Celia* (giggles): For a laugh?

*Rosalind*: Yes, for fun. C'mon, let's go!

*Celia*: Uh-oh, wait. Look who's stalking us. He's been spying on us from the doorway, listening to every word we say.

That's me she's talking about – the fat bloke

in the corner. Anyway, you get the picture. Celia's the one with fair hair. Rosalind is dark – a bit too skinny for me. I like them with some meat on their bones.

I'm meant to tell Celia to go see her dad, Duke Fred, short for Frederick. But I'm only a low-brow comic and I guarantee she won't listen, not with the crowd beginning to arrive for the big fight.

Look at that guy, Le Beau, talking to them now. Fancy clothes, fancy words – yack-yack-yack! Whoa, and there goes one of the poor saps who Killer just beat to a pulp – he's holding his head and moaning. And now Duke Fred and a whole bunch of celebs make their appearance. See the cameras flashing. They'll be in all the gossip mags next week with their bling and their Botox. I'll be there, too – at Duke's shoulder, feeding him one-liners to crack a smile on that sourpuss face. It's a job, and I'm paid to do it.

'You know we were talking about fit boys,' Roz says to Celia. 'Look over there. Who's *that?*'

She points to Orlando, who's schmoozing with the crowd. I might have known she'd fancy him. He's stripped to the waist for wrestling.

'How cool is he!'

'Very cool,' Celia agrees. 'But he won't stand a chance against Killer. Go tell him – quick!'

Roz runs up to Orlando in a panic. 'Hold on a second!'

Celia backs her up. 'If you get in that ring with Killer, you'll be mangled. Look at the size of him!'

'Speak to the hand,' Orlando replies, or words to that effect. 'I don't care what happens to me, and nobody else does, either. I'm all alone in the world.'

'*We* care!' Celia and Roz insist.

It's amazing what an effect blue eyes and a naked torso can have. The girls are putty in Orlando's hands. But Orlando climbs in the wrestling ring anyway.

*Clang*! The bell sounds and the first bout starts.

*Ouch*! Killer head-butts the Kid, who staggers back against the ropes. Now Killer's pinned him down on the canvas and he's thrashing about like a fish on a line.

*Och*! *Ouch*! Killer is raising his fist and he's about to crush the Kid, big time, just like he promised Oliver he would.

But what do you know! The Kid wriggled neatly out of that one and Killer is caught off guard. The crowd is cheering the Kid on. He's stronger than he looks. He sidesteps, and now he's got Killer in an arm lock. He's kicking his feet from under him.

*Oof*! Killer's down! Yes, he's down, and the Kid jumps right on top of him. He squishes him and knocks his head against the floor.

Duke Fred lifts his hand to say it's over. Killer Karl is down and out. They're carrying him off semi-conscious. His brains are mashed potato. Would you believe it!

'Good fight,' Duke tells the Kid. He asks him his name.

'Orlando de Boys.' The Kid's breathing hard, but there's not a mark on him. 'Roland de Boys was my dad.'

Duke frowns. 'Your father and me have unfinished business,' he says. And instead of smiling and giving the Kid the winner's belt and prize money, he stalks off with his crowd of hangers-on.

Like I said earlier, this place is a hotbed of feuds and gang fights. Oliver and Orlando, Roz's dad, Duke Senior and Celia's dad, Duke Fred. But I notice the girls don't go off with Fred.

'I'm sorry about my dad,' Celia says to Orlando. 'Don't listen to him.'

And Roz goes further – she takes off her necklace and hands it to him. 'It's all I have to give, but it's yours.'

Orlando is stuck for words – he just stares at her. The girls are leaving, but Roz is glancing over her shoulder. Now look – she's coming back!

'Did you say something?' she asks hopefully.

Orlando shakes his head. He beat Killer Karl in the ring, but one glance from a pretty girl and he's struck dumb!

The girls are leaving for good now and Orlando's sidling towards me, since I'm the only one left. I'd better give him a piece of good advice, so I don't have him on my conscience, such as it is.

'Get out of here quick,' I tell him. 'Now Duke Fred knows who you are, he'll mark your card – you know what I'm saying?' I make a slashing gesture across my throat.

'Why? What did I do?'

'It's not what *you* did, it's what your father did to him before he died. It made them sworn enemies. Fred is still looking for revenge.'

18

'OK, thanks. But right now I'm more interested in the girls. Who's the dark one?'

'You don't want to know.' I shake my head.

'Who *is* she?' Orlando insists.

I'm not about to argue with a guy who just pummelled Killer to the ground, am I? 'She's Duke Fred's niece. Rosalind's her name, and she's in the same boat as you, in that Fred hates her dad. Her old man is alive, but he's been kicked out into the Forest of Arden with a group of cronies. They've had to ditch the party lifestyle. No big mansions, no gas-guzzlers for them any more. They've gone green.'

'Stop!' Orlando tells me. 'I only want her name, not her whole life story!' Then he dashes off, sighing like a dumb-ass, lovelorn kid. Which he is.

Now back to the girls. Roz is moping around again. I overhear her tell Celia that the young wrestler threw her good and proper – and she's not talking arm locks!

'Do you really have the hots for Orlando?' Celia asks. 'I admit he's a hunk, but you've only set eyes on him once.'

'Once is enough,' Roz sighs.

'Ah! Love at first sight. But don't tell my dad. Duke looks like he's in a bad mood.'

It's time for me to fade into the background when I see the frown on Fred's face.

'You!' he yells at Roz, the second he spies her. 'Pack your stuff and go at once!'

'Me, Uncle?' she gasps.

Personally, I've seen it coming for a while. Rosalind puts Celia in the shade, she's so stunning and in-your-face. Fred doesn't like to see his own daughter down at number two in the eligible list.

'Yes, you!' he snarls. 'Get out of here, quick.'

'B-b-but why?' Roz never stammers, but she does now. 'W-w-what have I done?'

'Cut the Little Miss Innocence stuff. I don't

trust you as far as I can throw you. You're your father's daughter – that's enough!'

'No!' It's Celia's turn to challenge her wicked old dad. 'You can trust Roz, Pa – I swear on my life! She and I are joined at the hip – we were in the same class at school, we go everywhere together.'

'More fool you,' Fred sneers. 'She's conning you into thinking she's your friend, just so she looks better beside you in the paparazzi shots. She's taller and better looking, but you're too stupid to notice.'

That's a tough comment from father to daughter. Even I wince to hear it, and I'm pretty hard-boiled.

'If she goes, I go,' Celia mutters, but Fred doesn't believe her.

'You're history!' he tells Roz. 'And if I catch you hanging around here after this, you're dead!'

That's it – finished! He and his crew storm off.

21

'I meant it,' Celia whispers to Roz after the dust has settled. 'I'm not staying here without you.'

Roz shakes her head. 'You can't throw away your whole future just for me.'

'Yes, I can. You're my best friend in the whole world. Who's going to separate us after all we've been through and what we mean to each other? I promise – I'm coming with you!'

'But where?' For once, action-girl Roz doesn't take the lead. She's too upset.

'To Arden, to find your father, my uncle.' It's Celia who comes up with the bright idea.

'It's too dangerous,' Roz insists. 'We're just two spoiled little rich kids. We'd attract the wrong sort of attention.'

'Not if we dress casual and take off the bling.'

At last Roz gets her brain in gear. 'You're right! Especially if I dressed as a boy. I'm tall and skinny – I could so get away with that.'

She swaggers about with her shoulders thrust back and her legs wide apart.

Celia grins. 'That's better! What shall I call you?'

Roz thinks for a minute. 'Call me Jamie. And I'll call you Summer. Jamie and Summer, a brother and sister on their gap year – how cool is that?'

'Way cool, and maybe I can talk to Touchstone and get him to come along, too!'

That's one bright idea too many for one day, young Celia. Why would I want to leave the lap of luxury to rough it in the forest with you? It's time for me to vanish.

'Let's go and get ready!' I hear Celia add. 'Hey, this is going to be some adventure. Freedom, here we come!'

# Act Two
# Exile Arbour

26

Change of scene, but it's still me, Touchstone, providing the voiceover. Imagine the *Big Brother* commentator – the chatty bloke with the Geordie accent: *Day 22 in the forest, and Jaques has come to Exile Arbour to make his video diary…*

Jaques is one of Duke Senior's gang and fancies himself as a bit of a comedian. But he's not up to my level of razor-sharp wit. More sarcastic and glass half-empty, you might say. Always looks on the dark side.

'Hi, Big Brother, Jaques here. It's been nonstop in the forest since my last video diary. We've had a while to settle in now and Duke Senior and the rest of us have been fitting in well with local ways. Check out the long leather boots and foresters' tunics. And Duke Senior has taken to wearing a cool, feathered hat while he gives us a bit of a lecture – the old boy can't help it.

'"This exile experience isn't nearly as bad

as I expected," is what he said earlier today. "As a matter of fact, I *like* going green."

'"Embracing the Good Life?" his buddy Amiens asked with a shake of his head. He's hooked on the high life back in the city. "You mean you actually rate it?"

'"Yes." Duke Senior definitely means it. "What you see here is what you get. No one puts on an act. Even the bad weather is real."

'I couldn't believe what I was hearing. But then there's no fool like an old fool.

'"As individuals, we can learn a lot if we put our minds to it," Duke Senior said, going preachy on us. "Like how to be self-sufficient and hunt and kill a deer for supper, for instance."

'You could see he was up for it – tracking the poor beast and turning it into meat for our table. But don't hold your breath!

'Well, anyway, that's me done. I suppose I'd best get out of here and see how Duke Senior's getting on.'

See what I mean? Jaques never cracks a smile. And yet it's laugh-out-loud funny, seeing them all chase the poor deer until they're knackered, and then they *still* go hungry. Zilch for supper – not even a teeny-weeny bunny to put in the pot. Plus Jaques, Amiens and Duke Senior have no idea that two new groups are about to enter the forest – yes, that's right, *two*!

The first is headed by someone who hit the headlines earlier this week when he scored a major victory in the wrestling ring over Killer Karl. You already know him – the amazing Kid Orlando! He had to make a quick exit from town to keep out of Duke Fred's and his brother's way. You already know that Oliver is one mean guy. Orlando has someone you haven't seen before tagging along with him. I'll do the intros – this is Adam, an old guy who used to work for Orlando's dead dad. Faithful old Adam, still going strong.

The second group is made up of two major celebs and some fat bloke in the corner.

Did you guess? Yes, it's me and the girls, we're entering the forest as I speak! And listen, I may come across as pretty rough and out for number one, but I'm not that bad once you get to know me. Plus I've got the added excitement of having Roz and Celia here with me in disguise.

You won't recognise the girls. Roz is in drag, for a start – narrow trousers, loose white shirt, and with her hair cropped even shorter than before. And Celia's given up the Gucci bags and gone way downmarket to the Pound Shop. They're wandering into the forest like lambs to the slaughter, bless!

'I'm tired!' Roz-Jamie moans.

She's not the only one. I liked it much better where we were before, with all the creature comforts to make life bearable. But when she asked me to do the bodyguard thing for her and Celia-Summer, like a fool I agreed.

OK, I know what I said before. So I changed my mind! Don't look at me like that. And don't go digging for deep motives, because, believe me, there aren't any.

'There's no point complaining,' Celia-Summer insists. 'We're here now and there's no way back.'

'I'm so tired I could weep,' Roz-Jamie groans. 'But I'd better not do the girlie stuff while I'm dressed like this!'

'I know, we'll have to be mega careful. You can bet your life my dad has sent people after us to drag me back home.' Celia's got it all figured out.

'Why? What did you see?' Roz is a bag of nerves, jumping when a leaf so much as flutters in the breeze. And there's plenty of leaves and plenty of breeze out here in the forest, believe me.

'I didn't see anything. But we have to try

and find help – a shepherd or someone.'

That's how Celia's been brought up – expecting a knight on a white horse to charge out of nowhere and rescue her.

'I'm not sure if they have shepherds around here,' I point out. 'Trees – yes. Look around you. Deer – yes. I've seen some. Sheep – no!'

'Let's look anyway.' Celia sails on regardless. 'We need to find somewhere to stay before it gets dark. We don't want to be out here all night.'

'OK, let's go,' Roz hurriedly agrees.

'After you,' I tell her, super polite. Even though I'm the official bodyguard, I'm not going first into those dark shadows. There could be wolves, lions, leopards – anything!

'No, after you!' she insists.

We're not happy. It's creepy in the forest, and I'm way out of my depth. Unlike my old mates Jaques and Amiens, who have been here in exile with Duke Senior for a good while. Look at them!

Amiens has always been able to pick out a tune on the guitar – acoustic, not electric these days, naturally.

"Under the greenwood tree – la-la!" he sings. It's a song to fit the mood of the forest, about sweet birds singing and everything being love and peace, man.

'Spare me the hippie stuff,' sour-faced Jaques pleads. 'I've been hearing it all day from Duke Senior.'

Amiens sings another verse or two to wind Jaques up. 'Ambition's no fun,' he warbles. 'But lying all day in the hot sun and expecting nothing is where it's at – man! Live for the moment – give up all your possessions, blah-blah.'

'Don't give me that!' Jaques snaps, big time. 'Give me everything money can buy any day of the week!'

'Gotcha!' Amiens laughs, and goes off in search of his supper.

Now it's my turn to wind Jaques up as tight

as any clockwork toy, by playing him at his own miserable game.

So I'm lying in the sun minding my own business in a place where I know Jaques has to pass. He can't go by without poking his nose in.

'Hey,' he says. He doesn't recognise me because I've done the disguise thing, too, like the girls.

'Hey,' I answer, looking at my watch and sighing. 'Ten o'clock. An hour ago it was nine. In one more hour it will be eleven. That's how it goes – we ripen and ripen, then we rot and rot.'

For once in his life, Jaques laughs. He mocks me outright, calling me a fool for pretending to be deep about time and suchlike. He doesn't realise that I'm the one who's mocking *him*!

So anyway, Jaques runs straight off to Duke Senior and tells him he's decided he wants to be a real, proper, full-time comedian, because no one else gets the chance to speak their mind and not get punished.

Like when you stand onstage and deliver the punchlines, you can make fun of politicians and movie stars, and no one sues you for slander! And besides, there's no one in the world who doesn't deserve to be criticised. That's what Jaques says.

By now Orlando has had time to run away from the city, get lost in the forest and find himself again, but old Adam is worn out. Orlando gets him to a shelter then dashes off to find the poor guy something to eat, which is how he happens on Duke Senior sitting at his supper of boring bread and cheese, listening to Jaques ranting on about being a comedian.

'Stop right there!' Orlando cries, with Jaques in full flow. 'Hand over that loaf!'

Which changes the subject rapidly.

'That's pretty rude,' Duke Senior chunters. 'Breaking in like that.'

Orlando remembers his manners and says sorry but he's starving, so the old man pulls out a seat at the table.

It takes a big-hearted guy to make this kind of offer and it catches Orlando off guard, so he backs down completely. 'Sorry. I thought you'd be rough and ready out here in the forest,' he explains, 'so I planned a quick snatch and grab. It's so I can feed my friend.'

'Where's your friend now?' Duke Senior asks.

You're not likely to find anyone more open and generous, even though he does go on a bit. The duke's a one-off, he really is.

'In a shelter nearby,' Orlando replies. 'He was too old and weak to go any further.'

'Which proves there are others on the world's stage much worse off than us,' Duke Senior insists. 'Bring your friend here. We'll save food specially for him.'

So Orlando dashes off to fetch Adam, and Jaques launches into one. A BIG one, so pay attention:

'*All* the world's a stage,' he proclaims, 'and we're mere actors. We have entrances and exits written into the script. And one man plays many parts throughout his lifetime – seven to be exact.'

No one interrupts. Maybe they're too busy stuffing their faces.

'First we play the role of the infant – crying and puking in our mother's arms all day long.

'Then the schoolboy, our faces scrubbed, creeping at snail's pace through the school gates.

'Then we play the lover, sighing and writing bad poetry, which we dedicate to our girlfriend's eyebrow.

'Then a soldier with the heavy-duty swearing and the scruffy beard. A man living on a short fuse, going out there to win a medal in the face of enemy fire.

'Next comes the judge at our court bench, well fed and dishing out justice.

'On to the sixth age – an old man in slippers and trousers hanging off our skinny frames. Even our voices lose the deep, manly tone and slide up the scale a feeble octave or two.

'And then the seventh and last age – second childhood and nothingness – *sans* teeth, *sans* eyes, *sans* taste, *sans* everything.'

*Sans* is poncey Jaques-speak for 'without'. It's French. Just thought I'd fill you in.

You already knew that? Sloanes, like Jaques, the lot of you!

Jaques's voice falls away after '*sans* everything', and there's a morbid silence.

Thanks for that, Jaques, my old mate.

And just then Orlando comes back with faithful Adam, who's ancient and kind of gives the lie to Jaques doom and gloom about going ga-ga in your old age.

Duke Senior makes room for Adam at the

table then asks Amiens to play a tune to cheer everyone up.

Amiens does his best, but it's not a good choice of song – all about winter winds blowing and what false friends can do to you.

Duke Senior drifts off and asks Orlando a few quiet questions. When he finds out that Orlando is Roland de Boys's boy (get it?), he's over the moon.

'Your dad was one of my best friends!' he cries.

Orlando's grin spreads from ear to ear.

'Come into my cave!' Duke Senior tells him. 'I want to hear all about your life and how come you ended up in the Forest of Arden!'

# Act Three

# She Loves Me,
# She Loves Me Not

So now we're cookin'! Everyone's where they need to be to make this work – namely in the forest. But don't forget the mafia boys back home.

Duke Fred doesn't like to lose – not even a game of snooker. So when he hears that the Kid has made a getaway, he leans on Oliver big time.

He pots a red and then a colour, rests on his cue and chalks the tip. 'So, what's with your kid brother?' he asks, throwaway style.

Oliver is already sweating under pressure. He knows he has to let Fred pot the next ball. 'No news,' he mumbles. 'I haven't heard from him lately.'

Fred blasts another couple of reds and colours into the pockets. No way will he let Oliver off the hook. 'That's what I'm saying – what's with your little bro suddenly vanishing off the face of the earth?'

'Don't ask me,' Oliver shrugs, feeling the heat from the overhead lights.

'But I *am* asking you. No, I'm *telling* you!' When Fred turns nasty, it's not pretty. He gets this cold snake look in his eyes. 'I'm telling you to track down the boy and bring his head to me on a plate.'

Oliver's up against it, but he tries to laugh. It comes out as a croak.

'I'm counting on one-hundred-per-cent effort on your part here,' Fred goes on, missing the next ball. 'But, hey, no pressure, my friend!'

'Ha!' Oliver miscues and loses four points.

'Orlando's head on a plate, and every penny he owns into my bank account by this time next week,' Fred leans over the table, and this time he easily sinks the red.

'No problem,' Oliver promises. You don't say no to Fred – not ever, no way!

Not that Orlando knows anything about the price on his head. He's too deep in the forest and *way* too deep in *lurve*!

And I'm watching his every move.

Here he comes, pinning naff love letters to tree trunks, would you believe?

'Hang there,' he sighs, straightening the paper so everyone can read the poem he's written for Roz. Back home he'd probably go into a music studio and record a song – 'I love you true-oo, yes, I do-oo!' Out here in the wild, he has to make do with notes stuck on trees.

Whoops, there he goes again. And just in time – because here comes Jamie-Roz.

'Hey, Touchstone, what's that you're reading?' she asks me. She's feeling more at home in Arden now. Celia found herself a friendly shepherd after all, and the girls have a roof over their heads.

'I'm reading rubbish,' I tell her, acting like I'm going to tear Orlando's poem down and screw it up.

'Give it here,' she insists. And reads:

*'My heart is blowin' in the wind*

*For it belongs to Rosalind.*
*In my head and in my mind*
*I know that I love Rosalind.'*

She stand there gobsmacked by this galloping, country-and-western garbage. Or like she's been stung by a bee and is having an allergic reaction.

'A five year old could do better,' I tell her.

'At least it rhymes – nearly!' she grins, getting over the shock. To give her some credit, she's gone red with embarrassment and hasn't noticed Celia tearing down another of Orlando's poems and reading it out loud:

*'The world's a desert,*
*My heart is hurt,*
*Until I find my own true love –*
*Until I find my own true love!'*

'Not another!' Roz tunes in at last. 'How uncool is that? Who on earth is writing these things?'

Celia shrugs. 'They're all really geeky,

aren't they? And they're stuck up all over the place.'

'Do you recognise the handwriting, coz?' Roz demands. 'You do! I can tell by your face – you know who's written them!'

'God, Roz, you're slow!' Celia laughs. 'Ama-azing that you don't get it! Come on, dummy – think!'

'I *am* thinking!' Roz wails. And she jigs about impatiently. 'It's not fair! Tell me who it is!'

'A guy,' is the short answer.

'Thank goodness for that! But more information, *please*!'

Celia's enjoying this, but finally decides to put Roz out of her misery. 'OK, I'll tell you. It's that kid who floored Killer Karl earlier this week, and you, too, remember?'

'Be serious!' Roz gasps, turning white as a sheet.

'I *am* serious. It's him – Orlando.'

**47**

'Orlando!' It takes a while for this to sink in. 'Oh, no! What am I supposed to do now I'm in the Jamie disguise? When did you see him? Did he say anything? How did he look? Where did he go? What's he doing here? Did he mention me? Where is he now? Did you arrange to see him again? Answer me, quick!'

'Whoa!' Celia acts like a horse is galloping straight at her. 'Give me a chance. I saw him lying under a tree, sighing and talking to himself...'

'What was he saying?'

'Sshh!'

'Sorry! But you know me – I always speak without my brain in gear.'

'Listen. Orlando was under a tree – sighing, like I say. And then... Hang on a sec – here he comes now!'

Just in time, the girls spy Orlando taking a stroll with my mate Jaques. Quick as a flash, they hide behind a tree. Yeah, I know – the hiding behind the tree convention is a bit lame, but it happens here anyway.

'What are you doing, shadowing me like this?' Jaques asks.

'Me shadowing you? It's the other way around!' It's clear Orlando hasn't a lot of time for old misery guts.

Jaques gets right in Orlando's face. 'And while we're at it, quit sticking those feeble, adolescent love poems on the trees, OK!'

'Or what?' Orlando looks as if he's in two minds whether to wrestle Jaques to the ground there and then.

'Every single one is made out to a girl called Rosalind – it's a rubbish name, if you ask me.'

'I didn't!'

Jaques is so thick-skinned that he doesn't pick up signals about when to back off. 'Take my advice – forget her. She's not worth it.'

'Yatter-yatter-yatter!' Orlando mocks. 'Listen – I'm sick of you, d'you hear?'

'Not as sick as I am of you,' Jaques sneers, making his exit just before Orlando finally snaps.

Roz has overheard every word. Her eyes are sparkling. 'I'm going to keep up the Jamie disguise and have some fun,' she tells Celia. 'Watch this!'

Celia and me cringe as she steps out from behind the tree, right in front of Orlando.

'Have you got the time?' she asks in a cheeky-chappie way.

And here's the joke – Orlando doesn't even recognise the girl who stole his heart! He hasn't a *clue* who he's talking to.

'I'm not wearing a watch,' he mutters. 'Out here in the forest I lose track of time. Anyhow, where did you spring from?'

'Never mind about that. I don't think we've met before.' Roz-Jamie is faking well, except she hasn't put on the voice to match. 'I live with my sister on the edge of the forest.'

'You don't sound like a country kid,' Orlando says, passing the time of day.

'Not a local yokel?' Roz-Jamie grins. 'That's because I had an uncle from the city who taught me how to speak proper. He was kicked out for mixing with the wrong people and by the time I knew him he had a big chip on his shoulder and he was totally anti-women.'

Roz-Jamie and Orlando are leaning against a tree like old friends now – arms crossed, chewing the fat. Celia and me are creased up over it.

'What did he tell you about the opposite sex, this uncle?' Orlando asks.

'That women are all identical, like the five-pence pieces in your pocket, and worth just about as much.'

'Huh. So what happens when you fall in love with one of them?'

Roz-Jamie puts on a face like she's just realised something. 'Hey, are you him – the dude who's writing all these love poems?'

'Guilty,' Orlando admits. 'Now, go on – how would you recognise a guy in love?'

'Let me see – my uncle said that lovers can be made out by their thin cheeks and the shadows under their eyes – which you don't have. Also, when you're in love, you're not meant to shave and you don't care what you wear – any old thing will do. But that's not you, either. You're kitted out to look pretty cool, in my opinion.'

'No, believe me – I'm totally in love!' Orlando springs in front of Roz-Jamie, roughly six inches from her face.

Celia has to stuff her sleeve into her mouth to stop from laughing out loud.

'You're mad!' Roz-Jamie cries. 'Love's an illness. They should lock you up – I mean it!'

'So cure me,' poor Orlando begs. 'Go on – how would you do that?'

Roz-Jamie takes a deep breath. She knows she's pushing things a bit far now. 'I'd do some role play,' she tells him. 'I'd pretend to be your girlfriend and you'd have to woo me – just faking it, OK? Then every time you tried to flirt with me, I'd go all sulky and changeable. You wouldn't know which way I was going to jump. Sometimes I'd be all sweetness and light. Sometimes I'd be proud and shallow and stupid. One day I'd say I love you, the next day I'd hate you. I'd cry then I'd spit and drive you to distraction until all love was drained from your heart and so you'd be cured! Da-dah!'

Orlando shakes his head. 'What if I don't want to be cured?'

'Ah, but I could do it, I swear. Just try calling me "Roz" and come over to my place every day and see how you get on.'

Orlando laughs at her/him/her. Are you following this gender-bending action?

'OK, it's a deal.' He decides he's got nothing better to do. 'So, where do you live and how do I get there?'

It's one thing to jump with both feet into a game of faking it, another to carry it all the way through. Roz got carried away back there and now she's regretting it. And this is after only one visit from Orlando.

'Leave me alone. Let me blub in peace,' she tells Celia.

'Boys don't blub, remember!'

Roz sniffs, then tries to take control and block out her feelings for Orlando. 'OK, so he's not that good-looking.'

'Pretty ordinary, actually.' Celia agrees.

Roz acts like she's been stung. She drops the act. 'What are you saying – "ordinary"? Orlando's drop-dead gorgoeus!'

'Totally...'

'Apart from that, back to the serious stuff. Why did he swear he'd show up again this morning, and then not come?'

'He's totally unreliable.' Celia is deadpan through all of this.

'Really? You think so?'

'Yeah. No way is he in love. He only hangs out in the forest because he's mates with your dad.'

'Dad!' Roz is pulled out of her misery for a split-second. 'You know I bumped into him yesterday and he didn't recognise his own daughter! But anyway, about Orlando. Don't you think he's the dreamiest thing you've ever seen?'

So (*big sigh here from me*) she's got tangled up in her own game-playing, has Roz, and Celia's not about to help her get untangled – no way, José!

# Act Four

## He Loves Me,
## He Loves Me Not

To hear me natter on, you'd think the complicated Roz-Orlando romance was the only thing on the boil in the forest, but no way.

I haven't mentioned Corin by name yet, have I? He's the shepherd we're staying with, the girls and me. I get on with him pretty well, considering we've got nothing in common. Corin's a simple sort with a basic, no-frills outlook. For instance, he doesn't do the kissy-kissy greeting thing we do in the city because he says he's never sure how long it is since the other person had a wash, and I reckon that's fair enough.

'I'm a plain man,' he says, looking me in the eye. 'I work hard and earn an honest wage. I'm not a jealous type, either, and I don't waste time longing for what I know I can't have.'

I like that and I like him.

Better than his young sidekick, Silvius, whose mind isn't on the shepherding lark.

Silvius is too busy dreaming about some girl called Phebe, whispering her name and carving hearts on the barks of trees.

But Phebe's a cold fish and doesn't feel the same about him. In fact, she sent him packing. And here's a twist – Roz heard *her* giving poor Silvius the hard word and he/she told Phebe off, which was like stepping into a minefield.

'What right do you have to treat Silvius like that?' Roz-Jamie demands. 'You're not exactly super-model material. It's not as if you can afford to be picky.'

And what's Phebe's reaction? You've got it! She laps up the insults and begins looking at Roz-Jamie in a certain way. Yes, *that* way!

Whoa! Roz-Jamie tells Phebe straight that she doesn't fancy her, but Phebe's not the type to listen, so watch this space.

Are you following this? I know, it's *worse* than a soap opera, and there's more to come.

For instance, there's Audrey the goat herder – bless! Now Audrey's a farmyard disaster of a girl and doesn't have two brain cells to rub together. And the proof of this is that she fancies *me*! Yeah, really!

This doesn't happen to me every day, so I have to grab my chance while it's staring me in my fat face. Check this out!

'Touchstone, do you love me?' Audrey's covered in straw from the stable and is giving off a strong *eau de goat* pong.

'I love you so much, even the world's best poetry couldn't express it!' I say, sliding my arm around her wide waist.

'What's po-etry?' the poor girl wonders.

'Erm – it's how lovers speak!'

'And am I ... po-etical?'

'Very, Audrey, very!' I try to get my hands on more of her poetical girlie curves.

And then, as luck would have it, a country vicar, complete with dog-collar wanders by, and I grab him and beg him to marry

Audrey and me on the spot. And it's only old misery-guts Jaques who puts a stop to these hurried proceedings by telling us to find a church and do it the decent way.

So there you are – I'm an almost-married man, and Roz and Orlando aren't the only couple coupling!

Meanwhile, back at the ranch ... *cue, sound of galloping horses...*

What I really mean, is – back to Roz-Jamie, who's currently conning old Jaques with her disguise.

'You intrigue me,' he tells him/her in his plummy voice 'You *in-treeegue* me!'

Roz-Jamie cleverly steers the subject back towards old Jaques himself, giving him the chance to spout about why he's always so depressed – '*deep-ressed*!'

'I worked a long time to achieve this level of *deep-ression*!' he says proudly. 'It doesn't come easily. I have to work at it.'

Luckily, for all our sakes, Orlando is

nearby, with Celia hanging back in the bushes.

'Hi, Roz!' he breezes, before Jaques can blanket the world in his *deep-ression*.

Jaques does a confused double-take – as in 'Boy or girl? What is this?' – then leaves in a hurry.

'I'm not talking to you!' Roz-Jamie pouts at Orlando. 'You call yourself my boyfriend, but I've been hanging around here for an hour!'

'Sorry I'm late.'

'If it happens again, consider yourself well and truly chucked!'

'Roz, my Roz – don't be angry.'

Roz-Jamie switches her mood in a flash. 'OK, start chatting me up,' she says, leaning back against a tree. 'It feels like I'm on holiday – nice and relaxed. Go ahead.'

'Can I start with a kiss?'

Roz-Jamie jumps back out of reach. 'No! Talk to me, tell me something nice.'

'I'm lost for words,' the poor bloke stammers.

'OK, so I'll go first – I don't fancy you!'

'Then I want to die!' Orlando turns on the melodrama, just like that.

Roz-Jamie frowns in his face. 'Listen – the world is millions of years old, and we die of nasty diseases and by walking under a bus. But no one ever died for love!'

'Whoa, that frown looks way too real!' It's Orlando's turn to back off.

'Sorry,' Roz-Jamie mutters. 'I'll try to be gentler. Ask me anything – I'll say yes.'

'Then, love me, Roz!'

'OK. On Fridays and Saturdays.'

'Will you have me as your boyfriend?'

'Yeah, along with 20 others.'

'Listen to me. I want to marry you!'

'Will you, Orlando, take Rosalind as your wife? To have and to hold... Blah, blah.' She charges through the marriage service.

Now they're standing like they would at

the altar and it's affecting the hairs at the back of my neck. He's saying, 'I, Orlando, take thee, Rosalind...' Blimey!

She snaps out of it just in time. 'And how long will you stay faithful?' she challenges.

'For ever!' Orlando promises.

Roz-Jamie doesn't believe him. 'Promises, promises! Men always say that *before* they get hitched, but it's all downhill after that. After the wedding, I'll start to get jealous and I'll rant and rage. I'll cry for no reason and laugh at stupid jokes on the TV, especially when you're desperate to get some sleep.'

'Really?' Orlando grits his teeth, then jumps out of the role play. 'Are all women like that? Listen, I'd better make tracks. I promised Duke Senior I'd swing by his place for lunch.'

'Huh.' Roz was enjoying herself way too much. She's genuinely sad to see him go. 'Promise you'll be back by two?'

'Definitely.'

Orlando's on his way but she calls him back. 'Do you mean it?'

'I'm as serious as if you really truly are my Roz!' he insists. Then he's gone.

'You shouldn't have said all that.' Celia isn't happy. She overheard the stuff about girls growing jealous and crazy and making their guy's life a misery. 'You can't generalise and put us all down!'

'I didn't mean it,' Roz sighs as she fiddles with her fingernails. Then she looks up and comes clean with how she's feeling. 'I really, really love him, Celia!'

'Maybe you do – maybe not.' Celia shakes her head.

'I *do*,' Roz insists. 'I can't bear it when he's not here! In fact, I'm going to sit in the shade and dream about him until he returns.'

'And I'll take a nap,' Celia yawns.

Time drags when you're in Roz's frame of

mind. It's the old saying about the watched kettle never boiling.

*Tick-tock. Tick-tock.*

Roz is looking for Orlando in every shadow. She hardly notices when wimp Silvius shows up to deliver a letter from Pheebs. He has to shove it under Roz's face before she pays him any attention.

'Listen to this,' Roz tells Celia. 'To paraphrase: Phebe says I'm ugly and a chav, and she could never, ever love me!'

Celia smiles. 'Read it out properly!'

'*I put you on a pedestal and you stole my heart.*'

Silvius is earwigging and he's confused. 'That doesn't sound like she thinks you're ugly and could never love you!'

Roz reads on. '*You're so arrogant and up yourself, it's not true.* See!'

'Read some more,' Celia says.

'*Even so, I can't stop myself loving you.* Huh. Yes, you're right, she's still stuck on me.'

Roz turns on the messenger boy. 'But, silly Silvius, why deliver this letter? Don't you see Pheebs is trampling all over you? No way would I let her treat me this way!'

'Sshh, don't be so mean!' Celia feels sorry for Silvius, but he runs off without saying another word.

I've got another old kettle saying for you. The one about the pot calling the kettle black. In other words, Roz is the pot and Silvius is the kettle. See if you can work it out...

Confused? OK, I'll tell you – they're both in love and they're both acting like idiots!

Anyway, along comes someone we haven't clapped eyes on for a while – Orlando's big bro, Oliver. He's a mess though – unshaven and shambolic, like a football manager whose team has just been relegated. And for a while we don't recognise him.

'Bo-ooo! Get 'im off!'

No heckling from the audience, please!

'Hey, you two,' Oliver spies Roz-Jamie and Celia-Summer. 'Can you tell me where there's a shepherd's cottage surrounded by olive trees?

'West of here,' Celia-Summer tells him. 'In the next valley, by a row of willows. But there's no one home right now.'

Oliver is staring hard at Roz-Jamie and Celia-Summer. He mutters something that I don't catch. Then he asks, 'Do you two live there?'

Celia-Summer nods.

Oliver turns to Roz-Jamie and pulls out a hankie covered in blood. 'Orlando asked me to give you this. He says he's sorry he's late.'

'What happened?' Roz-Jamie cries.

'Let me explain,' Oliver says. 'Orlando was walking through the forest to Duke Senior's place for lunch when he came across a beggar lying under a tree, fast asleep. It was lucky for the tramp he did, because Orlando spotted a snake winding itself around his neck, ready to strike, so he beat off the snake and it slithered away.

'But that's not all!' Oliver has more to tell. He holds up his hand, warning Roz-Jamie to zip his/her mouth. 'Worse – under a nearby bush, a lioness was hiding. Once the snake left, she was ready to pounce. So Orlando ran and woke the tramp – and guess what, he found it was his older brother!'

'Oliver? We've heard about him,' Celia-Summer frowns. As you know, she never bad mouths anyone, but she doesn't hold back here. 'He's vicious and mega-mean!'

Oliver takes this without flinching. 'I *know*,' he mutters.

'But what about Orlando?' Roz-Jamie is desperate to know. 'Did he walk away and leave his brother to the lioness?'

'Almost,' Olilver admits. 'But no, he's too much of a hero for that. Instead, he turns and fights the lioness to save his lousy brother.'

'And how do you know all this?' Celia-Summer asks.

Oliver looks her in the eye. There's a big, dramatic pause. 'Because I *am* that brother.'

'The one who tried to have Orlando killed in the wrestling match?' Celia's mouth falls open.

'Yes, but don't judge me over that. I've changed – honestly!'

'What-about-the-blood-on-this-hankie?' Roz-Jamie almost screams.

'I'm coming to that. So anyway, Orlando soon finishes off the lioness and we catch up with what's being going on in each of our lives. I'm saying sorry to him like there's no tomorrow. And thanking him for saving my life. Then he takes me to Duke Senior's place and it's only then that we find out my kid brother is hurt. In fact he goes into a faint, he's lost so much blood! We patch him up, naturally. And when he comes round, he hands me this hankie, saying, "Give this to the young shepherd called Roz."

'"Roz"? I ask him. How come a lad has got a girl's name?

'Orlando nods. "It's a joke – a game we're playing. But take the hankie and give it to him."'

Now, guess what. Roz-Jamie does the girlie thing and falls down in a dead faint!

Celia-Summer drops down beside her and pats her cheek. 'Roz... Sorry, Jamie, wake up!'

'Don't worry. A lot of people can't stand the sight of blood,' Oliver says.

'There's more to this than meets the eye,' Celia-Summer tells him.

Then Roz-Jamie groans and wakes up. 'Take me home!' she whispers.

'Come on, toughen up,' Oliver says. 'Be a man!'

'Ha-ha!' Roz-Jamie makes a poor job of trying to laugh. 'Be sure to tell Orlando how well I played the girlie role!'

'Down to the deathly pale face and the shakes,' Oliver notes.

'Yeah, I'm pretty good at role play!' Roz-Jamie gasps as Celia-Summer drags her to her feet. 'Make sure you tell him that!'

'Anything else?' Oliver asks, helping Celia-Summer and Roz-Jamie back towards our cottage. 'I'll carry whatever message you want to send.'

# Act Five
# He/She Loves Me!

The beauty of this situation is, you can read it whichever way you like. It's up to you. 'As You Like It' – see!

You can say, *What's happening here? How come big bad Oliver has suddenly turned into Mr Nice Guy? It's not logical. It doesn't make sense.*

Or you can say, *It's only a rom-com, stupid. None of it matters, as long as there's a happy ending. At least four weddings and no funerals.*

I've just been fighting Haystacks Audrey off again. She's still dead set on marrying me, so there's a fair chance I'll be one of the weddings.

Right now I'm keeping out of her way and listening in on Oliver and Orlando.

'Hey, bro, are you sure about Summer?' Orlando is quizzing. 'You hardly know her. You've only seen her once. And yet you're telling me you're head-over-heels in love with her, even though she's only a poor country girl with no money whatsoever!'

'I know, I know.' Oliver realises it looks all wrong. But he's a changed man and he's been struck by Cupid's arrow – *ping*! 'I've told her how I feel, and Summer swears she feels the same way.'

When did this happen? I hear you ask. Yeah, it's very sudden, and it takes some swallowing. Affairs of the heart are like that, y'know.

'So I've decided to stay here in the forest with her and give Dad's luxury pad in the city back to you,' Oliver says with a flourish.

Orlando grabs the offer with both hands. Who wouldn't? 'OK, I'll sort out the wedding for tomorrow. I'll invite Duke Senior, Amiens, Jaques and the rest. You go and tell Summer it's all fixed.'

That's wedding number one, if you don't count me and Auds! And here comes the making of number two – Roz-Jamie shows up just as Oliver rushes off to give Summer the good news.

'Hey,' she says to Orlando, taking a deep

breath and acting casual.

'Hey,' Orlando replies.

'How's the arm? I see you've got it in a sling.'

'The arm's good, thanks.'

'Did Oliver tell you how I faked a faint when I heard the news about the lion?'

Orlando nods. 'I was impressed. Plus he told me about him and Summer getting married. How cool is that?'

'I know! *Your* brother and *my* sister! Love at first sight. I saw it with my own eyes. There they were, falling into each other's arms and swearing to be true before anyone had time to turn around.'

This all happened offstage. Roz and I saw it, though.

'I'm over the moon for them,' Orlando says. 'But them being happy makes me think how deep-down upset I am about Rosalind. Listen, Jamie. Do you mind if we call off this role-play stuff?'

'I know – it's getting too hard. So, OK.' Suddenly Roz-Jamie goes into a different gear. Not so flippant any more. 'I'd like to help,' she tells Orlando. 'And I know this sounds far-fetched, but I'm in touch with a guy on the telly who does magic tricks – he's quite famous, actually. I'll talk to him. And I promise he can use his magic to get you and your Rosalind together.'

Orlando is gobsmacked. 'You mean it?' he stammers.

'Trust me,' she insists. 'You dig out your designer threads and get dressed up tomorrow. Invite all your mates to Summer and Oliver's wedding. I'll wave my magic wand – da-dah! I'll make your dreams come true, and I swear you and Roz will be married, too!

They're staring into each other's eyes and I'm going goose pimply when Phebe and Silvius march in.

She strides up to Roz-Jamie and gives

him/her a shove. 'That's for showing Silvius the letter what I writ you!'

Roz struggles free. 'Silvius loves you, you idiot!'

'I do!' he swears.

'And I love you, Jamie!' Pheebs doesn't give in easily.

'And I love Rosalind!' Orlando sighs. He's got it bad.

'And I don't love any woman!' Roz-Jamie declares.

'I'll never look at another woman!' Silvius tells Pheebs.

'Me, neither!' Pheebs throws her arms round Roz-Jamie's neck.

'Me, neither!' Orlando pictures Rosalind in his arms.

Roz-Jamie struggles free. 'Me, neither,' she mutters.

Now Silvius goes off on one. 'Being in love is like a fairy tale, where wishes really *do* come true. I adore you, Phebe, and I'll wait for ever, whatever you do, wherever you are!'

'Stop, please!' Roz-Jamie makes a gagging noise. 'It's worse than hearing a wolf howl at the moon. Listen, Silvius – I'll help you if I can. I'll just say this – get ready to be married tomorrow!'

Roz-Jamie turns from Silvius to Pheebs. 'Phebe – I'd love you if I could, and I'd marry you if I ever married a woman! Now, believe me when I say that you'll get married tomorrow, too!'

Then she turns to her love. 'Orlando, I'll make your dreams come true, and I promise you'll be married tomorrow.

'Meet at Oliver and Summer's wedding, everyone!'

'We will!' they cry.

What a set up.

What a finale!

Meanwhile, a small musical interlude occurs, to show that time is passing. All the best romcoms have them. If I was the director, I'd be filming birds warbling in trees and water dancing in sparkling streams.

Cue, guitars and tambourines:

*Love is in the air*
*Sweet love*
*Yeah, ring-a-ding-ding!*
*Roses in the air*
*Sweet smell*
*Yeah, ring-a-ding-ding!*
*Spring is in the air*
*Sweet spring*
*Yeah, ring-a-ding-ding!*

I know – it's rubbish! But hey, what did you expect?

OK, so now it's the Big Day. Duke Senior is asking Orlando if he thinks Roz-Jamie can deliver on his/her promises. Celia-Summer's keeping quiet in the background.

'Fingers crossed,' Orlando says as Roz-Jamie puts in an appearance with Pheebs and

Silvius. Roz is still cross-dressing, remember.

'I just want to check something,' Roz says hurriedly to Duke Senior, her dad. 'If I can produce Rosalind here in the forest, do you promise to let her marry Orlando?'

Duke Senior swears he will.

Roz then double-checks with Phebe. 'And if you change your mind about wanting to marry me, do you promise to get hitched to Silvius instead?'

'It's a deal,' Pheebs agrees.

'OK, I'm out of here!' Roz-Jamie says, then dashes off with Celia-Summer.

For a second or two, I think Duke Senior is about to rumble Roz-Jamie. 'Call me crazy,' he mutters to Orlando, 'but that lad reminds me a bit of my daughter!'

'Funny you should say that,' Orlando replies. 'I had the same idea when I first came across him, here in the forest.'

I step up with Audrey and take their

minds off Rosalind, so as not to spoil her grand entrance.

'Can I join in the wedding-fest?' I ask. 'I've done all the romantic build-up and Audrey says, yes, she'll marry me. She may not be much to look at...'

Audrey pulls down her frock, gives a wriggle and shows too much cleavage.

'Act more seemly, Audrey!' I hiss. 'Er-hum! And I've fought off all my love rivals. Killed 'em stone dead. So, what do you say, Duke?'

Duke Senior has no time to answer before the wedding march begins and – da-dah! – Rosalind and Celia march behind the marriage lady in their designer wedding dresses. Here come the brides!

'Remember what Jamie told you?' Rosalind says to Old Duke and Orlando, showering them with smiles. 'Is this magic, or what?'

There are loud, puzzled cries from the guests. 'Roz?' 'Jamie?' 'Were they really the same person?' 'Wow, what a cool disguise!'

The couples, including me, are hugging and crying for joy, except Pheebs, who looks as if she's been struck by lightning.

'You're my only father,' Roz tells Duke Senior. 'And you're the only husband I'll ever want!' she says to Orlando.

You gotta have respect for the girl, and the way she's pulled it off.

'Is everybody here?' the marriage lady asks, clipboard at the ready. 'All the couples must hold hands. Now, Orlando and Rosalind, Oliver and Celia, Phebe and Silvius, Touchstone and Audrey, step forward to be married!'

Four weddings!

We all stare into each others' eyes and swear to honour each other for ever. Ah!

Then we line up for the wedding photos, and we smile and grin. All, that is, except misery-guts Jaques, who can never crack a smile even though he's just heard news from the city that Fred has done a U-turn and chucked in the whole mafia business.

Yes, that's right – another surprise. Duke Fred's decided to hand the family business back to Duke Senior and turn to religion instead.

So Duke Senior has got his money back and now can't wait to leave the forest. Back to the limos and the jacuzzis. So much for going green.

'I'm off to join Fred and become a monk,' Jaques announces.

Exit one sourpuss and failed comedian.

We newlyweds are all too happy to pay much attention to him. We're dancing and singing, partying like there's no tomorrow.

We leave it to Roz to make the wedding speech.

'Thanks, everyone, for coming,' she says, raising her glass. 'I hope you're all enjoying yourselves. Now, party on!' Short and sweet.

We all hold up our glasses and toast the brides.

And that's it from me, the fat bloke in the corner. Everything worked out well, didn't it? Ta-ta!

# About the Author

Jenny Oldfield was born in Yorkshire and lives there again after a spell in the Midlands, where she read English at Birmingham University.

First published at the age of 24, she has had her *Home Farm Twins* series adapted for BBC television, and has written more than 100 books for adults and children. Her work, including *Horses of Half Moon Ranch*, is available in the UK and America, plus translations into many European languages

Whilst teaching in a school in Brimingham, Jenny directed a version of *As You Like It* with a talented group of young actors. She enjoyed the experience so much that this chance to adapt the play came as an offer she could not refuse...

# SHAKESPEARE TODAY

William Shakespeare's

AS YOU LIKE IT

Retold by Jenny Oldfield

# SHAKESPEARE TODAY

WILLIAM
SHAKESPEARE'S

*A Midsummer Night's Dream*

RETOLD BY

ROBERT
SWINDELLS

# SHAKESPEARE TODAY

WILLIAM SHAKESPEARE'S

# Macbeth

RETOLD BY
**TONY BRADMAN**

# SHAKESPEARE TODAY

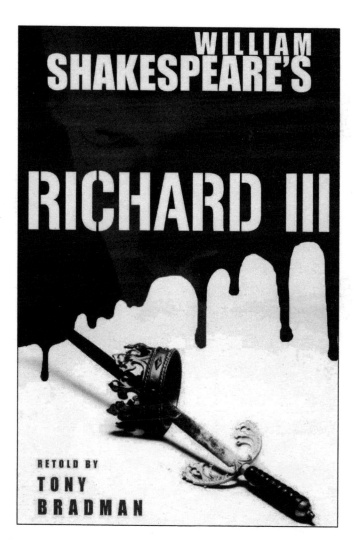

WILLIAM
SHAKESPEARE'S

RICHARD III

RETOLD BY
TONY
BRADMAN

# SHAKESPEARE TODAY

WILLIAM SHAKESPEARE'S

*The Tempest*

RETOLD BY
FRANZESKA G. EWART

Also by Louise Doughty

**ff**

*Apple Tree Yard*

Yvonne Carmichael has a high-flying career, a beautiful home and a good marriage. But when she meets a stranger she is drawn into a passionate affair. Keeping the two halves of her life separate seems easy at first. But she can't control what happens next.

'There can't be a woman alive who hasn't once realised, in a moment of panic, that she's in the wrong place at the wrong time with the wrong man. Louise Doughty, more sure-footed with each novel, leads her unnerved reader into dark territory. A compelling and bravely written book.' Hilary Mantel

'Doughty is a superb storyteller who knows how to build suspense to breaking point.' Kate Saunders, *The Times*

'Doughty has a particular gift for unsettling stories, for making us ask difficult questions of ourselves, our own relationship choices, and this is her strongest book yet . . . entirely compelling.' *Observer*